This book belongs to

sidneyMiller

Tangled

A Read-Aloud Storybook

ADAPTED BY CHRISTINE PEYMANI
ILLUSTRATED BY JEAN-PAUL ORPIÑAS, STUDIO IBOIX,
AND THE DISNEY STORYBOOK ARTISTS

 Random House New York

Copyright © 2010 Disney Enterprises, Inc. All rights reserved. Published in the United States by Random House Children's Books,
a division of Random House, Inc., 1745 Broadway, New York, NY 10019, and in Canada by Random House of Canada Limited, Toronto,
in conjunction with Disney Enterprises, Inc. Random House and the colophon are registered trademarks of Random House, Inc.
Library of Congress Control Number: 2010923935
ISBN: 978-0-7364-2718-0
www.randomhouse.com/kids
Printed in the United States of America
10 9 8 7 6 5 4 3 2

Once upon a time, there was a beautiful golden flower with magical healing powers. Only the selfish and vain Mother Gothel knew where it grew. For centuries, Mother Gothel used the flower to preserve her youth.

One day, the beloved Queen became very sick. Desperate to save her, the whole kingdom searched for the magical flower and brought it back to their Queen. After drinking a potion made from the golden bloom, she quickly returned to full health. Soon the Queen gave birth to a beautiful princess. To celebrate, the King and Queen launched a floating lantern into the night sky.

Furious, a withered Mother Gothel sneaked into the castle nursery. When she hummed the song that had made the flower's magic work, she discovered that the baby's golden hair glowed—and turned her young again! She cut a lock of the hair, planning to take it with her. But the hair instantly stopped glowing and turned brown. Mother Gothel realized that the only way she could remain young was to keep the child with her always. Before the King and Queen could do anything, Mother Gothel snatched the Princess and vanished into the night.

Mother Gothel fled with the child, Rapunzel, deep into the forest and locked her in a secret tower. Everyone in the kingdom searched for their princess, but they could not find her. The King and Queen were heartbroken.

Each year on the Princess's birthday, the King and Queen released lanterns into the night sky. They hoped their light would guide their princess home.

Many years passed. Mother Gothel raised Rapunzel as her own daughter. Since there was no door in the tower, Rapunzel would lower Mother Gothel to the ground with her long golden locks, and pull her back up.

Rapunzel spent her days painting, knitting, doing laundry, brushing her hair, and keeping busy with other chores and activities. She was happy to have the love of Mother Gothel and the companionship of her only friend, Pascal the chameleon. But there was one thing Rapunzel desperately longed for—to leave the tower to see the floating lights that appeared every year on her birthday.

On the day before her eighteenth birthday, Rapunzel asked Mother Gothel to take her to see the floating lights. Mother Gothel refused, insisting that the world outside was full of scary things like thugs, quicksand, and snakes. It was far too dangerous a place for a weak and helpless girl like Rapunzel.

Meanwhile, in another part of the forest, a thief named Flynn Rider was on the run. He had just stolen something valuable from the palace with the help of his cutthroat partners, the Stabbington brothers. Flynn clutched a satchel tightly as he came to an abrupt halt in front of a WANTED poster of himself. He thought he looked much more handsome in real life.

By Order of the KING
WANTED!
1,000 CROWNS REWARD!

THIEF

As soon as he had a chance, Flynn left the Stabbington brothers behind. They were too dangerous to be trusted. Flynn took off alone with the satchel. He was able to elude the palace guards, but a horse named Maximus was determined to catch him. Maximus chased the thief onto a tree at the edge of a cliff. *SNAP!* The tree broke and Flynn and Maximus tumbled into a canyon below.

Landing safely, Flynn ducked into a cave to hide from the horse. When he emerged on the other side, he saw a beautiful hidden valley—the very valley where Rapunzel's tower stood!

Flynn thought the tower looked like the perfect place to hide from Maximus. So he quickly scaled the tower wall, using arrows like a ladder. When he finally reached Rapunzel's window, he climbed inside.

CLANG!

Startled at the sight of a stranger, Rapunzel hit Flynn with a frying pan! Then she dragged him to a cupboard and locked him inside.

Besides Mother Gothel, Flynn was the first person Rapunzel had seen since she was a baby. But he didn't seem at all like the scary ruffians her mother had warned her about. In fact, Flynn was very pleasant-looking.

Rapunzel felt exhilarated by her encounter with the stranger. Surely this act of bravery would prove to Mother Gothel that she could handle herself in the outside world.

Rapunzel found a strange object in Flynn's satchel. It was round and gold, with sparkling jewels. She placed the object on her head and was amazed to discover that it was a perfect fit!

"Rapunzel! Let down your hair!" Mother Gothel called from the bottom of the tower. Rapunzel quickly hid the gold object and pulled Mother Gothel up.

Rapunzel decided to ask Mother Gothel again if she could see the
floating lights. She was about to show Mother Gothel the stranger in the
closet, but Mother Gothel cut her off.

"Enough with the lights, Rapunzel!" she shouted. "You are not leaving
this tower, EVER!"

For the first time, Rapunzel realized that Mother Gothel intended to
keep her locked in the tower forever! She knew she had to come up with
a plan to see the floating lights. Rapunzel quickly told Mother Gothel
that she had changed her mind. Instead of seeing the lights, she wanted
special paint for her birthday. Even though it would take a three-day
journey to find the paint, Mother Gothel was relieved and agreed to
Rapunzel's request.

Rapunzel dragged Flynn out of the cupboard and tied him to a chair with her hair.

"Do you know what these are?" she asked, revealing a painting she had done of the lights.

"You mean the lantern thing they do for the Princess?" asked Flynn.

"Tomorrow they will light the sky with these lanterns," said Rapunzel. "You will act as my guide, take me to the castle, and return me home safely. Then and only then will I return your satchel."

"Fine, I'll take you to see the lanterns," Flynn agreed, desperate to get his satchel back.

As Flynn climbed down the side of the tower, Rapunzel paused at her window. She had been waiting for this moment for nearly eighteen years, and now she didn't know if she could really leave. But with Pascal on her shoulder, she took a breath and slid down her hair, all the way to the bottom of the tower.

For the first time ever, Rapunzel felt the soft green grass beneath her feet.

"Woo-hoo!" she exclaimed. She felt ecstatic—but also guilty. She knew Mother Gothel would never forgive her for disobeying her.

Meanwhile, as Mother Gothel traveled through the forest, she ran into Maximus. The palace horse was still furiously searching for Flynn. Mother Gothel rushed back to the tower, terrified that the King and Queen had found Rapunzel at last.

Mother Gothel entered the tower through
a hidden door. She searched every inch of
every room, but Rapunzel was nowhere to be
found. However, Mother Gothel did find the
satchel with the crown and Flynn's WANTED
poster. She was convinced that the thief had
kidnapped Rapunzel. At once, she set out to
find them.

Eager to get his satchel back, Flynn suddenly
had an idea. He would frighten Rapunzel back
to the tower! So he took her to a pub called the
Snuggly Duckling.

When they stepped inside, there were
menacing thugs everywhere.
Rapunzel was so scared, she
couldn't utter a word.

"Hey, you don't look so good, Blondie," said
Flynn, trying to sound sympathetic. "Maybe
we should get you home and call it a day?"

But Flynn's plan backfired. The thugs recognized him from his WANTED poster and started fighting over who would turn him in for the reward. Rapunzel scrambled up to the top of a table and banged two pots together.

"Put him down!" she demanded. "I need him to take me to see the lanterns because I've been dreaming about them my entire life! Haven't you ever had a dream?"

"I had a dream once," said one of the thugs softly. In fact, all of the thugs in the pub had dreams of their own. They understood what Rapunzel was going through and wanted her dream to come true. So they let Flynn go.

Suddenly, the castle guards burst into the pub with the captured Stabbington brothers. Flynn was sure he would be arrested—until one of the thugs showed them a secret door that led into a tunnel.

"Go live your dream," the thug told Rapunzel.

Flynn and Rapunzel ran as fast as they could through the underground tunnel and skidded to a stop at the edge of a cliff. Maximus, the royal guards, and the Stabbington brothers were right on their heels! Rapunzel lassoed a rock with her hair, swung through the air, and landed on a rocky ledge.

Flynn fought off Maximus and the guards with Rapunzel's frying pan! Rapunzel threw her hair to Flynn and held on tight as Flynn leaped off the cliff and swung right over the heads of the Stabbington brothers!

But Rapunzel and Flynn hadn't escaped yet. A dam suddenly burst, filling the cavern with water!

A huge wave washed Maximus, the guards, and the Stabbington brothers away. Flynn and Rapunzel ducked safely into a cave. But a stone column crashed to the ground and trapped them inside.

Water rushed into the cave! Flynn cut his hand on a sharp rock while searching for a way out. "It's no use. It's pitch-black, I can't see anything," he said.

"This is all my fault," Rapunzel said. "I'm so sorry, Flynn."

"Eugene," said Flynn. "My real name is Eugene Fitzherbert. I thought someone should know."

Rapunzel decided to share a secret of her own. "I have magic hair that glows when I sing." And that was when she realized—her glowing hair could light their way out!

Meanwhile, Mother Gothel had found her way to the Snuggly Duckling. She had seen Rapunzel and Flynn escape into the tunnel. When one of the thugs emerged from the pub, she forced him to tell her where the secret tunnel let out. She went there and waited for Rapunzel and Flynn. But to her surprise, it was the Stabbington brothers who emerged.

"I'll kill that Rider!" shouted one of the Stabbingtons. Hearing that, Mother Gothel came up with a wicked plan. She offered to help the brothers get revenge on Flynn, as well as obtain something even more valuable than the crown—Rapunzel's magical hair! With the help of the Stabbingtons, Mother Gothel would trick Rapunzel into coming back to the tower willingly.

Soon Rapunzel, Flynn, and Pascal were safely back in the forest. Rapunzel wrapped her hair around Flynn's wounded hand. As she began to sing, her hair began to glow. Within moments, Flynn's hand was completely healed.

"Once it's cut, it loses its power," Rapunzel said, trying to explain her hair's magic. "It has to be protected. That's why—"

"You never left the tower," Flynn guessed.

Rapunzel nodded sheepishly and then quickly changed the subject. "For the record, I like Eugene Fitzherbert much better than Flynn Rider," she said with a smile.

When Flynn left to gather firewood, Mother Gothel burst out of the forest. She was eager to take Rapunzel home. But Rapunzel refused.

"You don't understand. I met someone," she said.

Mothel Gothel told her that Flynn was only using her to get the crown back. Before returning to the forest, Mother Gothel handed Rapunzel the satchel and dared her to give it to him.

Rapunzel thought she could trust Flynn, but she was also afraid of losing him. She hid the satchel in a tree before he returned.

The next morning, Rapunzel awoke to hear Flynn crying for help. Maximus was dragging him away! Rapunzel quickly stopped the horse.

"Today is kind of the biggest day of my life," she explained, patting Maximus on the head. "And I need you not to get him arrested—just for twenty-four hours."

Flynn held out his hand. Maximus pondered for a moment and then offered his hoof. The two shook on their truce.

Hearing bells in the distance, Rapunzel climbed to the top of a hill. The entire kingdom was spread out before her! Rapunzel was awestruck by the beautiful sight. She couldn't wait for the best day of her life to begin! She sprinted down the hill, with Flynn, Maximus, and Pascal close behind.

The hustle and bustle of the town was the most exciting thing Rapunzel had ever experienced. She couldn't wait to see and do everything. First, a little boy gave Rapunzel a kingdom flag with a sun symbol on it. Then a group of little girls braided Rapunzel's locks and pinned them up with flowers. Now Rapunzel wouldn't have to worry about people stepping on her hair.

"Thank you!" Rapunzel exclaimed.

With her hair out of the way, Rapunzel followed the crowd to the town square. When Rapunzel saw a mosaic of the King and Queen holding their baby girl, she was mesmerized. The baby princess had emerald-green eyes—just like her own.

A dance honoring the lost princess began. Rapunzel and Flynn joined hands and were quickly carried away by the music. They whirled around the square, laughing and enjoying each other's company.

Next they ventured off to explore the town. Rapunzel tried on a beautiful dress, ate cupcakes, and made colorful chalk drawings on the street. It was the most perfect day she could ever have hoped for!

As night fell, Flynn led Rapunzel to a boat and rowed them to a spot where they would have a perfect view of the lights. Rapunzel sat quietly, deep in thought. "What if it's not everything I dreamed it would be?" she asked.

"It will be," Flynn reassured her.

"And what if it is?" Rapunzel asked. "What do I do then?"

"You get to go find a new dream," he told her.

Soon, hundreds of lanterns illuminated the sky. Flynn handed Rapunzel her own lantern. In return, Rapunzel took out the satchel she had been hiding all day and gave it to Flynn. She was no longer afraid he would leave her once he had the crown. Flynn tossed the satchel aside and reached for her hand. The two gazed into each other's eyes. Everything around them seemed to fade away as Flynn caressed Rapunzel's cheek. They leaned in closer until their noses were just about to touch. . . .

Flynn suddenly backed away.

"Is everything okay?" asked Rapunzel.

Flynn had spotted the Stabbington brothers on the shore. "I'm sorry, there's something I have to take care of," he said.

Flynn left Rapunzel in the boat and went off to see the Stabbington brothers.

"The crown is all yours," Flynn told the brothers.

"We heard you found something much more valuable than the crown. We want her instead," said one of the Stabbingtons.

Then the brothers knocked Flynn unconscious and sent him out into the harbor tied to the helm of a boat.

Rapunzel was just starting to get worried when the Stabbingtons walked up to her. They told her that Flynn had traded her and her magical hair for the crown. Rapunzel could clearly see Flynn steering a boat away from them. She called out to him, but he didn't respond.

Rapunzel couldn't believe that Flynn had betrayed her. As the Stabbingtons lunged for her, Rapunzel ran into the forest. Unfortunately, her hair got caught on a tree branch.

As she frantically tried to free herself, Rapunzel heard a scuffle. She looked back and saw Mother Gothel standing over the brothers, who lay unconscious on the ground.

"I was so worried about you, so I followed you," explained Mother Gothel. "And I saw them attack you and . . . Oh my, let's go before they come to."

"You were right, Mother," Rapunzel sobbed.

Mother Gothel smiled. Her plan had worked perfectly.

Flynn's boat hit the dock outside the castle. When he regained consciousness, he immediately called out for Rapunzel. He knew she was in danger. But before he could do anything, two palace guards found him tied up—with the stolen crown. They immediately dragged him off to prison.

Standing nearby was Maximus. He had seen everything. The horse knew he had to help Flynn escape.

In the jail, the Stabbington brothers were locked in a cell. They admitted that Mother Gothel had told them about Rapunzel's magic hair. Flynn now understood that Mother Gothel had tricked all of them to get Rapunzel back.

Just then, the thugs from the Snuggly Duckling burst in to rescue Flynn! They overpowered the prison guards and catapulted Flynn over the wall and onto Maximus's back.

"Max, you brought them here! Thank you," said Flynn.

The horse neighed and galloped at top speed through the closing gates. The heroes were off to rescue Rapunzel!

Back at the tower, Rapunzel lay on her bed, heartbroken. She held a kingdom flag in her hand—a souvenir from her magical day in the town. She looked at the kingdom's sun symbol on the flag and gazed up at her paintings on the ceiling. She noticed that the golden sun was everywhere! She had unknowingly been painting the symbol her entire life!

Suddenly, a series of memories rushed through her mind: the lanterns being released on her birthday; the mosaic of the King, the Queen, and the green-eyed princess; the crown she had tried on the day before. Rapunzel finally realized the truth.

"I'm the lost princess," Rapunzel declared.

Mother Gothel tried to speak, but Rapunzel wouldn't listen.

"You were wrong about the world, Mother. And you were wrong about me."

Mother Gothel pulled her arm out of Rapunzel's grasp and fell backward into a mirror, shattering it.

"I will never let you use my hair again," said Rapunzel, turning away.

Soon Flynn and Maximus reached the tower.
"Rapunzel! Rapunzel! Let down your hair!"
called Flynn.

The window opened, and
Rapunzel's golden tresses
fell to the ground. Flynn
began to climb.

When Flynn crawled through the window, Mother Gothel stopped him.

"Rapunzel was just saying she'd never let me use her hair again," she said. "Let's see if I can change her mind."

Mother Gothel pressed a dagger into Flynn's back and chained him to the wall.

Rapunzel was desperate to save Flynn. She begged Mother Gothel to allow her to heal him. In return, Rapunzel promised Mother Gothel she would stay with her forever.

Mother Gothel agreed to the bargain and let Rapunzel go to him.

"Rapunzel, don't do this," Flynn begged.

Rapunzel quietly placed her hair on Flynn's wound. "I'll be fine," she said. "If you're okay, I'll be fine."

She took a deep breath and was about to sing. At that moment, Flynn grabbed a shard of broken mirror—and cut off Rapunzel's hair! The golden locks instantly turned brown. The magic was gone!

"Nooooooo!" screamed Mother Gothel, gathering the precious hair to her. "What have you done?"

She gazed into the shattered mirror and was horrified at her reflection. Within seconds, she had aged hundreds of years and turned to dust.

Rapunzel grabbed Flynn's hand, pressed it to her short brown hair, and began singing. But nothing happened.

"Don't leave me," Rapunzel gasped. "I can't do this without you."

He reached up to touch her cheek and smiled. "You were my new dream," he murmured.

"And you were mine," said Rapunzel.

As Flynn closed his eyes, Rapunzel began to weep. A golden tear fell on Flynn's cheek and began to glow. Rapunzel stared in disbelief as light spread across Flynn's body. Then he slowly opened his eyes. He was alive!

Rapunzel, Flynn, Maximus, and Pascal journeyed back to
the castle. Rapunzel entered the empty throne room and waited.
When the King and Queen arrived, they paused for a moment,
stunned. The Queen reached out to Rapunzel and pulled her
close for a long embrace. Rapunzel touched her father's face as
he wrapped his arms around his wife and daughter. At long
last, the lost princess had come home.